EAGLES

LIONS OF THE SKY

Written by Emery Bernhard
Illustrated by Durga Bernhard

HOLIDAY HOUSE • NEW YORK

Thousand-year-old eagle carving from Mexico

Text copyright © 1994 by Emery Bernhard
Illustrations copyright © 1994 by Durga Bernhard
All rights reserved
Printed in the United States of America
First Edition

Library of Congress Cataloging-in-Publication Data
Bernhard, Emery.
Eagles : lions of the sky / Emery Bernhard ; illustrated by
Durga Bernhard. — 1st ed.
p.   cm.
ISBN 0-8234-1105-2
1. Eagles—Juvenile literature.   [1. Eagles.]   I. Bernhard,
Durga, ill.   II. Title.
QL696.F32B47   1994   93-1833   CIP   AC
598.9′16—dc20

The griffin is an imaginary animal
that is half eagle and half lion.

For Hilary and Ruth, our tireless librarians

Special thanks to raptor expert Tom Cullen for his comments on the text and artwork,
and to Dona Tracy of the Hudson Valley Raptor Center.

An African eagle soars high into the sky, spiraling toward the sun. Far below, a lion gazes lazily down from a tree. The eagle and the lion are patient, skillful hunters. Both are swift and fierce when they attack, and both make use of their sharp claws. Small antelopes grazing on the grassy plain watch out for the eagle and the lion.

MARTIAL
EAGLE

Just as the lion is said to be king of the beasts, ruler of all the animals on the land . . . the eagle is known as the king of the birds, the proud lion of the sky.

U.S. POSTAGE STAMPS

EAGLE IMAGE ON
U.S. PASSPORT

U.S. ARMY DRUM, 1860

Few people have seen eagles in the wild, yet everyone knows what an eagle looks like. The Bald Eagle is our national bird. It is found on many things, including coins, flags, dollar bills, postage stamps, military uniforms, and government buildings.

FIGURE WITH EAGLE HEAD
AND WINGS FROM
ANCIENT NEAR EAST

NATIVE AMERICAN EAGLE
ORNAMENT FROM
NORTHWEST COAST

THE GREEK GOD ZEUS AND HIS
EAGLE ON ANCIENT POTTERY

Thunderclouds build and lightning flashes, but the eagle calmly rides the wind. Since ancient times, the eagle has stood for the sun and the wind, thunder and lightning.

**WHITE-BELLIED
SEA EAGLE**

8½ FEET
MARTIAL EAGLE

3 FEET
LITTLE EAGLE

Eagles have wingspans ranging from 3 to 8½ feet. Eagles that fly over open country have wider wingspans than eagles that fly through forests.

Eagles are at home in the sky. Birds of prey, they search for food while flying or perching in high places.

Eagles stretch their wings to glide on the wind or to soar in spirals on rising air. An eagle may fly hundreds of miles a day, cruising along at thirty to fifty miles per hour and soaring up to 14,000 feet.

When the sun warms the earth, the air above open ground rises. The rising currents of warm air are called thermals (<u>THUR-mahls</u>).

Steady winds blowing against a hillside form updrafts. Eagles can glide on updrafts for miles.

Eagles have strong feathers at the tips of their wings that spread out like fingers. By moving their wing tips and their tails, eagles steer smoothly through the air.

With its large eyes, an eagle can see eight times more clearly than a human. It can spot a rabbit hopping in

Eagles have a special clear, thin eyelid that cleans and protects the eye. It is called a nictitating membrane (NICK-tih-tate-ing MEM-brayne).

the grass from a mile away, or track a shadowy snake slithering through jungle leaves.

Like other predators, the eagle hunts for smaller animals to eat. It often attacks weak and sickly animals.

CRESTED HAWK EAGLE

ISIDOR'S
EAGLE

Once it spots its prey, the
eagle plunges. It may dive at
speeds of two hundred miles per
hour, or float down slowly to catch
its dinner by surprise.
Just before it strikes, the eagle
thrusts its feet forward. Its toes
spread wide to seize its victim. Each
toe has a curved, razor-sharp talon.
If the animal is not killed instantly,

An eagle's talon
can be up to
4 inches long.

the eagle squeezes with its powerful
talons until its prey is dead.
Eagles usually carry their prey to a
nearby tree to eat. An eagle that
feeds on the ground may hide its
catch with its wings while eating.
Eagles use their hooked beaks to
tear flesh into pieces.

The Golden Eagle is the only booted eagle found in North America. It is also found in Africa, Asia, and Europe. It is the most common eagle in the world.

Eagles are found on every continent except ice-covered Antarctica.

There are about sixty kinds of eagles. They can be divided into four main groups: booted eagles, Harpy Eagles, snake eagles, and fish eagles.

The Harpy Eagle is found in Central and South America. It is the heaviest and most powerful of all eagles. It weighs up to 20 pounds.

<u>Booted eagles</u> have a thick covering of feathers on their legs. They hunt for small animals in mountains and woodlands.

<u>Harpy Eagles</u> live in the jungle and eat animals that live in trees, including monkeys.

The Bateleur (<u>bat-uh-LURR</u>) is a colorful snake eagle that hunts in the grasslands of Africa.

<u>Snake eagles</u> have stubby toes for grabbing snakes and strong beaks for breaking their backs. Protected by thick feathers and scaly legs, snake eagles can eat poisonous snakes without being harmed. They also eat lizards, birds, and fish. There are no snake eagles in North America.

The Bald Eagle is a fish eagle. It is not bald. It looks bald from a distance because it has bright white feathers on its head. The Bald Eagle is the only fish eagle found in North America.

<u>Fish and sea eagles</u> live near water. They have long talons and small spikes on their toes for gripping slippery fish. They sometimes steal fish from other birds of prey. When fish and sea eagles cannot find fish to eat, they will attack seal and sea otter pups, ducks, and geese.

Some eagles stay in the same place all year round. Others follow their prey as the seasons change. In the rainy season, tropical eagles may fly to drier areas. When ice and snow cover the land, northern eagles fly south to warmer areas or gather near a good food supply. This is called migration. Eagles may migrate thousands of miles every year.

Each winter, up to 4,000 northern Bald Eagles flock to the Chilkat River in Alaska to feast on salmon. Warm springs keep the river from freezing.

In spring mating season, eagles return to their old nests. When it is time to mate, male and female eagles who are not paired call to each other. Trying to attract a mate is called courtship.

Courting eagles may chase each other through the air, diving and looping. Sometimes, male and female eagles fly high and come together, grasping claws. With talons locked, the eagles fall. They cartwheel toward the ground. At the last moment they let go and flap hard until they are flying high again!

Eagles usually stay with the same mate for life.

After courtship, the eagles build a nest in a tall tree, on a cliff ledge, or in another high-up and out-of-the-way place. The eagles weave twigs and large sticks together. They line the nest with leaves, moss, grass, feathers, or pine needles.

Year after year, eagles add on to their old nest. They may also build a new nest that will be used if the old one falls down.

Fish and sea eagles build the biggest nests of any bird. Bald Eagle nests have measured 20 feet high and 8 feet across.

Soon after the nest is ready, the female lays one to four eggs. The eggs must be kept warm by the adult eagles, who take turns sitting on them. This is called incubation (<u>in-kew-BAY-shun</u>).

Eagles incubate their eggs for up to forty-five days. They warn strangers away from the nest and will fiercely defend the eggs. When the eaglet is ready to hatch, it cheeps inside its egg. Then the eaglet begins pecking a hole in the thick shell.

It can take as long as two days to break out of the egg.
A newborn eaglet is tired, wet, and helpless. It weighs
only three ounces. The eaglet sleeps for hours tucked
under its parent. By the second day, its coat of fluffy
down is dry. The hungry eaglet is fed tiny shreds of
meat by its mother. Its father is busy hunting for food
to bring back to the nest.

By nine weeks, most eaglets have shed their down coats and grown feathers. The eaglets play at attacking prey with their feet. They practice flying by hopping and hovering in the air over the nest.

Eagles are usually fully grown by four months. They glide out of the nest, flying for the first time. This is called fledging. Although young eagles may be fed by their parents for up to six months after fledging, most eagles learn to hunt for themselves after two months of flying. They often feed on prey that is already dead, called carrion (CAH-ree-on).

Eagles grow their adult feathers between the ages of one and a quarter and six years. Then they are ready to mate.

Eagle eggs and young eaglets
may be eaten by crows, raccoons,
and snakes. Young eagles can fall
out of the nest, crash on their
first flight, or starve.

Adult eagles have no enemies,
except for humans. They may live
for more than forty years.

Predators like the eagle keep down the numbers of small animals in the wild. Without predators, there would be too many animals and not enough food. Eagles also catch the mice and rats that destroy food grown by farmers.

Because birds of prey catch weak and sick animals, they prevent the spread of disease and help keep the whole animal population healthy.

As humans move into the wilderness, they cut down trees and poison the water and air. Small animals and fish take in the poisons, and so do the eagles that eat them. Eagles are shot, killed by the electricity in power lines, and caught in traps meant for other animals.

A century ago, there were twice as many eagles in the world as there are today.

Many of the great forests where the Philippine Eagle once lived have been destroyed. There are only a few hundred of this rare Harpy Eagle left.

But humans have also helped eagles. Governments have set aside land where it's safe for eagles to live. In some places, people have stopped polluting the water and air and no longer use pesticides. Wildlife experts have nursed injured eagles back to health and placed eaglets in the wilderness to help the eagle population grow. Power companies have built platforms where eagles can build nests.

Eagles were once thought to be brave, powerful, and wise. Native peoples in North America, Asia, and Africa often wore eagle feathers. They tied them onto their drums, rattles, shields, and lances. They carved and painted eagle symbols and performed eagle dances. When they wanted to be heard by the gods or spirits in the heavens, they called upon the eagle to carry up their prayers.

Long ago, Native Americans thought of the eagle as a brother. Today, every eagle still belongs to the family of living things. Can we learn to share our earth with the lions of the sky?

When we protect the environment on the earth, we protect the home of the eagle. We can all help make the world a place where eagles will always fly.

Glossary

bird of prey: A bird that kills and eats animals for food.

carrion (CAH-ree-on): The flesh of dead animals.

courtship: When male and female animals attract each other for mating.

down: Very fine soft feathers.

eaglet: A young eagle.

environment: The surroundings in which animals and plants live.

fledging: Taking the first flight.

migration: The seasonal movement of animals from one place to another for feeding or mating.

nictitating membrane (NICK-tih-tate-ing MEM-brayne): The clear thin eyelid that cleans and protects the eye of the eagle.

pesticide: A chemical used to destroy pests; it may also harm other animals.

predator: An animal that hunts and kills other animals for food.

prey: An animal that is taken by another for food.

talon: The claw of a bird of prey.

thermal (THUR-mahl): A rising current of warm air.

tropics: Very warm areas close to the equator.

updraft: Upward current of air formed by a steady wind blowing against a cliff or hillside.

EDUCATION

P

A